This is dedicated to all gay men.

I

As the knight stood before his brand new king; and he knelt; and he honoured; and he expressed his purpose; he finally learned, for the very first time, the real pleasure of submission.

Simon Hallow had seen armies raised and castles built, but neither compared to a king – for a king alone could rise from a golden seat to come and tip the chin of his loyal follower up to look him in the eye. And despite the monsters he slew and the witches he burned, Ser Hallow had certainly never seen armies nor castles tell him that they liked the colour of his eyes.

"The golden iris is a mark of the warrior," his majesty said.

The Keyholder Series
The Beautiful Man Without Mercy

Simon, awestruck once again by being drawn to witness the king's beauty, did all his best to simply nod. His mouth hung open and his eyes brimmed wide as he looked at his new liege with endearing rapture.

Great and good king Nicholas, first of his name and lord high protector of Draybury, stood above the new, kneeling knight at five foot eight. He did not dress the hedonist like most of his peers, instead the king wore simple garbs tied at the waist. Upon a closer look, one might see patterns embroidered into the brown fabric in a slightly softer colour that betrayed the real wealth and craftmanship that went into the garment; still it painted him classy. His boots too were nothing much prettier than a bard's, only differentiated like his tunic for the rich fastenings.

Of course that all paled in comparison to the mighty crown atop his hair. Mighty so that it needed no gems embedded – it simply sat there wrought in gold and edged in iron; a strong headpiece for a strong leader.

But when Simon at last managed to tear his attention away from the king's face – with his soft, pale skin and sharp mouth that turned up just slightly with amusement – he paid no attention to his clothing. For his eye was caught by none other than the crimson streak that highlighted his dark, black hair. It was black, unnaturally so, a feature contested only by its softness.

"Rise good ser." He commanded. Simon rose.

Despite being a good measure taller, he couldn't help but feel the king still towered over him. Nicholas may have been tight and reserved where Simon was muscular and wide, but that didn't stop the muscles under skin from shifting with every movement.

"Follow Vargo to your chamber. A position recently opened on my King's guard and I'd be glad to fill it with a man as eager as yourself."

The knight was from far up north, right by the wall that divided the seven kingdoms from the painted men. He had grown up fighting the border reavers, a task that built him into the warrior he was today. With his body of steel and eyes of great destiny, he knew he had to travel far from his small town of writers and historians to reach the kingdom that needed able men. And so he appeared, three months later, at The Dale.

It had a name once, but with spriggans moving in across the past centuries, the last remaining dale in Drayburyshire that still belonged to humans had been aptly renamed to just The Dale.

And that's exactly why Simon was so eager. With a strong king on the throne and spriggans to fight, he knew that Draybury would soon become the place for knights to be if they wanted their songs sung in the annals of history.

"Just this way," Vargo said. His voice, deep and rough, snapped him out of the king-Nicholas-induced trance.

Vargo was the court warlock when it fancied him. His appearance was the stark opposite of the young king – whereas he was but three and twenty, the magician was said to have been hundreds of years old. Although his body looked no younger, and certainly no more frail, than Simon's own. Vargo did, however, have black hair like the king but rather than a crimson streak, it had a gradient that fell down to the end of his neck from pitch black to whispers of ruby red.

He was tall as well, seven foot easily and just as wide as the knight. His loose robes betrayed the cleavage of his smooth chest and Ser Hallow wondered how someone could dress so casually before their grace.

And while Vargo was certainly living up to his middling reputation, this was not actually the first time Simon had met the man. On his way through the courtyard not minutes ago, when he arrived with his head held high, he had walked past many knights like himself. They were training in the yard, biting at dummies with steel blades in great discipline. He yearned to be like them soon, sweating at the brow to train up for their service.

It was a short-lived illusion broken by the appearance of a young man at his side. He was dressed in mail as the other knights yet he seemed to be much greener. He had come, as if from nowhere, to warn him apparently.

"Go, I beg you, go." Behind the boy Simon could see - only after he already felt the rumbling - an approaching man in robes of black that seemed to shimmer blue or purple at its own discretion. The large man with his lazy stubbled grin placed a strong hand on the boy's shoulder just as he said, "it is not worth it, go while you can!"

"Now, now, Joshua. Let's leave the good man be, eh?"

"V-Vargo," the green knight stammered, surprise painting his face. As he was lead away by the large man's muscled hand tight on his shoulder, the words in his eyes changed from 'run' to 'help.'

"Some men just aren't cut out for the job," Simon said in the present.

"Precisely," came the warlock's words as they stopped before a fine, wooden door. The knight noticed for the first time how the other man's teeth, just two near the front, were pointed into fangs. They weren't the sharp needle-like fangs of a bloodsucker nor the canines of a canine – they were *strong* points used for decimation rather than something as simple as eating or hunting.

Ser Harrow decided it best to remain on this man's good side and so said his thanks to the man with a bow at the neck. The warlock returned the gesture and headed back down the corridor the way they came.

What interested him most, as it turned out, between all the arcane personalities of the court warlock, was the big ring of keys that rattled silently at his hip. He had seen it once before as he turned away from him to lead the green knight and noticed it again now as he swept away. He saw it just between the fluttering slit that opened the hem of his shirt and when he looked again this time he managed to make out that, while they all appeared identical, each had something scratched along the metal. A word, he assumed, although it was too fast and too far to read.

When he looked back up he saw that the man was peering back at him with curiosity in his amber eyes.

"Oh, you'll learn about those soon enough."

"No, I didn't mean to-"

Vargo grinned, "yes you did. Staring at keys like this on accident... that's to come."

"Sorry?"

"You're initiation is soon. Until then... rest well." And he walked back down the stairs, disappearing into the darkness and leaving behind but a shadow that flickered and laughed in the torchlight.

Simon shook his head.

I am worthy.

He entered the given room and found that it was surprisingly cozy. His bed was made up with freshly cleaned, albeit a bit rough looking, linen. The only other proffered piece of furniture was the dresser pushed against the other wall. Besides that, it was stark but for the window. It was a nice window, however. Cast with swirling decorations, the glass may have pooled at the bottom but still it was gorgeous. And the sill was made of a fine piece of wood, clearly cut from the same log as the well-crafted door.

Simon moved, finally relaxing, to sit by this window sill and stare out at the midday sun. He saw the leagues of men like him still working hard at the training – sweating as they tore their muscles up. Across the castle walls he saw more guards patrolling and others standing sentinel.

The detail he admired most about the scene was the apparent dedication everyone had. They didn't just train their swordsmanship; they pushed as hard as they could. Their sparring matches were more than simple exercises; each was a hardened battle. He couldn't wait to be a part of it all.

He was about to head off then, to find the barracks, the stables and the dining hall, to induct himself into the castle ecosystem until his eye was caught by a small, white object. It was the corner of a piece of paper, flapping against the glass and slid in between the wood of the sill and the wall.

He slid his fingers against it, crumpling it, in his attempts to grab the corner until he finally managed to trap it under his nail and drag it out. What slid from it's hiding place was a letter written in hastily scratched characters.

Simon flattened it out against the surface and read the words illuminated by sunlight. As he did, they entered his mind as a black confession:

To whomever fills my station,

Know I did not leave it willingly. They will say I committed the crime. I will confess to having committed it too... but I was driven to it, I say. I'm writing this to tell you that I did, in unsound mind and body, sit on his majesty's throne. A crime like that was easy to punish with a beheading. And I'm glad for it, for it was freedom at last. Freedom from service. Freedom from him and his slavery. I implore you, great knight whoever you may be, to know that the cage is not worth the glory.

-Jon Tennant

Later, when touring the kitchen and meeting the staff, Simon chucked the letter in with the scraps of food waste where it would never be seen again.

For when he read those words and comprehended the former knight's meaning he decided one solid fact about himself right then:

I will never be that weak.

II

It was nice to feel the fresh morning air whipping at his face. After rising early to a simple breakfast of oats, Simon had taken to joining a few other knights out in the training yard. His own sword, Rogue, had been taken to the smith to be restored after it's harsh use during his journey; he now wielded a simple a broadsword borrowed from the barracks.

He wielded it well, though, and managed to keep up with the other knights of the king's guard – the only other men training this early in the morning.

After time passed with the climbing sun, the grounds soon filled out with other members of the order, ones who hadn't been assigned a patrol of some sort. Grunts filled the air to accompany the singing steel. A song was written in the atmosphere of hard exertion and broken straw dummies. A sort of natural synchronicity developed as the soldiers all battered their muscles together in a harmony rather like a dance floor. They went on like this, honing their bodies to be just as fine a weapon as their swords, right up till midday.

However early or late everyone arrived, the group all started funnelling out together around the same time to get their lunch in – hopefully something a bit more nutritious.

Another knight who was training besides Simon ended up complaining to himself, "lord, doesn't it get tight after training all day." He adjusted his crotch as another man joined him and agreed.

"Are you two alright?" he walked over to them both, hoping he could give assistance. He may have been new to the castle but he could tell just from a glance that his experience far outweighed both these men together.

The first knight, however, just looked confused, "uhm, yeah, it's just the- y'know."

"Man," the other knight said, "he hasn't been initiated yet."

"*Oh*. Should we tell him?"

"Nah," knight two answered with a sly look. He had a sharp face and cunning eyes below a shock of honey-brown hair. Simon would later learn, for better or for worse, that this man was Kyle Karn; a rather infamous member of the order.

"Yeah... yeah," the other knight replied.

"Come on, are we not brothers now?" Ser Hallow did his best to smile amicably. The first knight tried to awkwardly share his fervour but Kyle just sniggered.

"Not yet we're not."

"We're all knights to the same king."

"No," he said sourly. He walked up and jabbed a hard finger at Simon's chest, "there are the initiated and then there is everybody else. You know nothing of us."

The other knight piped up then, "h-he'll know soon."

All three men turned to see the captain of the guard approaching. An older man, but not any less built than the rest of them, with a garb that was indomitably black where everyone else's was white.

"With me, Hallow." He commanded, his voice sure. "Karn. Jackson. Go and eat." The other two mumbled obedience as they headed off with the rest.

The captain didn't bother to waste his breath on more unnecessary words, he just lead the way through the castle irregardless of whether or not Simon was following.

He chased, for the older man took big steps with his thick legs, and caught up to him in a hallway he had glazed over during his first visit.

Simon realised they were going to the throne room.

"Ah, ser, shouldn't I wash before I enter? I am rather disgusting after the morning's drilling?"

The captain walked on. Oh, he had heard Simon and Simon knew it. But he just kept on walking.

"Alright," he grumbled, still following obediently.

He at least appreciated that now he had time to admire the décor in this hallway. Yesterday he had arrived in the evening to fluttering cleaners and soldiers doing a shift swap that he hadn't properly seen the history weaved across the walls. It went on, oldest first from the entrance, all the way down to the throne room – to the present. Those earlier histories were told in woven tapestries. Later on they changed to epic paintings and soon large portraits.

At the end, where Simon had insisted they stop, he saw a large image of what looked to be King Nicholas but with a beard. The hair colour was wrong though. This man had handsome, chestnut hair.

"Captain," he implored, "who is this?"

The other man looked disgruntled by the interruption but soon softened, only slightly, when he saw the topic. He looked on the portrait with warmth in his eyes.

"That is Duncan III, father of our good king. The smaller portrait next to it depicts his regent."

Simon understood then. When he looked at the regent he saw a man with the same soft skin and jet black hair as Nicholas. Looking between the couple, he could see the way their features mixed to make the young man who ruled today.

His next question was going to be about the fact that Nicholas' blood parents were of the same sex, but apparently the Captain had decided to end the little tour and continue onwards.

Simon hurried and came to stand by the man's side just in time to reach the foot of the throne where the king sat oh so perfectly.

Jealous of a throne, Simon chided himself before he watched the king rise. He was dressed much more regally today, in colours of deep red and luscious cream. Around his shoulders was a thick and mighty cape befitting a monarch. Simon got down on one knee while the captain bowed at the neck.

"Ser Hallow. Trusting that you are willing, today will be your initiation into my sacred Order of the Knights of the Ram."

The Ram being the symbol of Draybury. A unique one, at that, for it was no heraldry but rather a symbol borne from the traditions of the people who lived there. The royal family adopted the logo and built great statues of rams across the county for people to pray to and children to play on.

It was a bond – *the* bond – between the monarch and his people.

It was tied together by his honourable Order of the Ram to mean an army that fights for justice rather than profit.

To reclaim the dales, it is always said.

"With me," the captain begun, "I'll-"

The king held a finger up. The captain was silent immediately.

"I will do this one myself," Nicholas announced, "I've been rather fond of the tales of his exploits. Do you remember The Lay of Ysard?"

The captain grunted, "I can't say I'm too familiar with verse, your grace."

The king ran his fingers through the cherry-blond hair of the knight before him. Simon shivered at the action, but did not dare move otherwise. He focused his attention of the boots of his liege, happy to be kneeling beside them.

"Let's just say that I was rather jealous of the king you served before me. I would like to cage you myself," he was talking down to Simon now.

He felt the heat rising to his cheeks but still dared not to remark.

"As you command," he heard the captain say before bowing again and taking his leave. Once the door was shut and Nicholas had removed his fingers from the knight's hair, he dared at last to look up, pleading in his eyes.

"Cage, your grace?" he finally uttered.

"I have a... policy. One that ensures my knights not only remain totally loyal but also determined to win." As he spoke, he thumbed a brown cord that was hung around his neck. It slowly teased out from under his collar to reveal a key, pretty and decorative, that hung at the end. Simon recognised it to be of the same design as those that hung at Vargo's waist.

"What must I do?"

"Everything," the king whispered. "Now stand." He did, coming up tall that he had to look down at his majesty though he still felt like the smaller one.

"What should I- ah ah!" His breath hitched as the king moved his left hand to cup Simon's manhood. It wasn't an aggressive gesture – he cradled him softly – but it was authoritative. It didn't anger or offend the knight, it just made him feel vulnerable; powerless. Like the king was only holding what rightfully belonged to him.

Nicholas moved his right hand to hold the key up between his fingers. Simon groaned as the grip on his body tightened or shifted – it was an involuntary noise that betrayed his fluttering stomach.

The king ignored him. He closed his eyes, took a deep breath in and tipped his head backwards a bit. The motion pushed his chest forward and caused his royal cape to slide off his shoulders. The new look allowed Simon to notice how his kingly garbs hugged his tight body. Who has the right to be so beautiful?

The whispering started next. A chant came from the king's soft lips, echoing in the wind around them. As he spoke, a ribbon of pure black tattoos began to wind themselves around him. They started at the wrist of each arm, snaking hidden under his sleeves before reaching the collar where they poked up to wrap around his neck. These tattoos continued to go up the king's face where they ended as they reached his eyes – eyes that opened the moment the tattoos were done.

During this procedure, Simon had felt a new tightness growing around his groin. When the other man removed his hand, the tightness remained.

Suddenly, Nicholas exhaled. As he gently recovered his breath, the tattoos swirling around him slowly faded into his skin where they disappeared leaving behind his usual marble complexion.

He let the key rest now on his chest as he moved the hand, just one finger, to tug at the edge of Simon's trousers.

"A-ah," he moaned, suddenly embarrassed and moving his hands to cover himself. The king didn't say anything, he just looked up at Simon, expressionless. He swallowed nervously at the look, that look of kingly expectation, and returned his hands to his side.

The king tugged the breeches and looked down at the result of his spell.

"Is it comfortable?" he asked.

What now covered the knight's penis was a shining, metal cage. It had a slit at the end and a ring at the other side that wrapped around his entire manhood.

"Yes, my liege." He meant it. It felt warm.

The king uncurled his finger and slowly tied the drawstring back, never breaking eye contact with his soldier.

"I look forward to working with you, good ser."

He walked off then, back out to his chambers, leaving Simon alone.

That feeling of warmth never left him though. It would never leave him, ever, in fact as that smooth cage always carried the slight, cradling heat of the hand of the man who now owned his cock.

 III

The plus side was that the cage itself never became uncomfortable.

The down side was that everything else did.

The physical feeling was just like a soft cradle with the tightness of the ring becoming commonplace by the end of the day.

No, it was the mental affect that Simon struggled with.

He hadn't been so desperately active that sudden cold turkey was debilitating for him, but he had enjoyed sampling his fair share of men before. Both low and high born, his taste was never too precise: he had that fling in his youth with the smith's brother who had publicly boasted on his heterosexuality; he had many sneaky moments with other knights in other barracks in other kingdoms; there was King Ysard; and there at last was a recent bard who he had become quite fond of before they parted ways.

But these were people he found closeness with. Brothers-in-arm and trusted men. He didn't sleep around and so a night of restriction was completely forgotten.

But then a second night passed and a third and at last a fourth when finally his groin had started to feel... *heavy*. Charged? He couldn't quite pin that feeling of need in his manhood but it was there and it was starting to make it harder to fall into slumber.

Day five went by and so did six and so did seven. Each night took him longer to get to sleep and each night his cock felt more desperate. He could no longer find a particularly handsome fellow soldier who's hand he could splurge his frustration into. There was no bush on the side of the road into which he could empty his troubles when he needed.

He was forced to pent up that tension until it spread right up to his head. It clouded his mind, making him restless, aggressive and worst of all, desperate. When people talked to him he bit back and when they tried to play nice all he perceived was mocking.

His late nights soon turned from hard efforts of forcing himself to sleep to needy hours grinding against his covers. He did always manage to catch a few hours but it was always with that little damp patch of pathetic, fruitless exertion staining his sheets.

It was twenty days since his caging when he finally let it all get to him. Out on the grounds, the biting steel of Rogue back in his hands, he hacked his way through straw. The tipping point was the fact that these training days and sparring sessions were his only reprieve from the frustration – only today they had stopped working. His lack of relief had numbed him so much that not even raw aggression could cure it.

That didn't stop him from trying. He cut harder, he stabbed harder he sliced harder and harder, battering away at the dummies across the yard. He hit again and as it did nothing to fix his problem he only hit again. He grunted louder as he did this until finally, in a deep shout, he cut diagonally through a dummy tearing it to pieces and leaving nothing but a sad pile on the floor.

Heaving deeply and profusely sweating, the rumbling sound of rushing blood in his eardrums finally ebbed away leaving him aware of his self at last. People were looking and Simon blushed for it, suddenly embarrassed and deeply ashamed of his actions.

After swallowing his nerve and calming down he finally realised that no one was laughing or mocking. As everyone else went on about their business, the knight realised that people were simply looking at him with pity.

"You doing alright, brother?" The man who came to rest a hand on his shoulder – bringing him back to focus – was very kind, Simon thought. He could tell just from his eyes; he was the kind of man that made a knight.

"Just having a hard time... y'know."

"Adjusting?"

"Yeah." He felt his cheeks redden slightly, still a bit embarrassed about the whole endeavour. While no one could see the cage, *he* could see that ever so slight distinction of the end of it forming a bump on his groin, however small and unnoticeable. And wearing it, constantly feeling it, meant he was constantly aware of his dick – a state of mind that no man should be in if he wishes to do anything productive. It made him feel naked, almost, despite the covering.

"Can I ask," he said to the other knight, "do, um, we all have one? Every knight here? I saw a few in the baths..."

The other man chuckled, "we do, we do. Everyone of us, even the captain. Vargo is the keeper of our keys. Well, except for that one his grace wears around his neck, oooo, I'd like to know who that belongs to."

Simon turned even redder, "me too, I suppose."

"Come on," the kind knight smiled, "it's bath night anyway so let's head there early."

"Why?"

"Because we're going to go and play every man's favourite game."

Simon soon learned that this peer was called Nathaniel. He quickly came to calling him Nathan for the fact he couldn't do with saying all that every time.

Nathan had lead him through the courtyards and out into the gorgeous marble building that made up the bathhouse. It was old, ancient even, a gift left behind from the Neroman's occupation of the island many ages ago.

They were rare in the country but the good king Nicholas was kind enough to give a weekly bath night to the soldiers he kept so diligently in line. Squires came in every day to fill the bath with clean, heated water so that his majesty may make use of it at his discretion.

When they reached the antechamber besides it for stripping down, Simon finally asked what this game they were playing was.

"I'll show you mine if you show me yours."

Any embarrassment he might have had was washed away by the fact he was trying his very best not to gratify Nathan with a smile.

He started to undress first and soon the other man followed suit until they were both completely nude.

"I'm glad to talk to someone about this, actually." He was trying his level best to ignore the way Nathan was ogling his locked penis. "I was starting to worry about, uh, hygiene."

Nathan shrugged, "don't worry about that, the magic takes care of you."

"Wow. Why does the king even keep Vargo about if he can do magic like that?"

A couple of other knights had started swarming in to change. The nudity was normal, a comfort even for male companionship. But a few had started to half-listen in.

"What do you mean?" Nathan asked.

"You know, when the king did the whole..." he explained by holding his hand under Nathan's balls to mime the cupping action of the spell.

"No," he said, crossing his arms, "Vargo put the spell on all of us."

"Oi, oi, what's this then!" More knights had come. From half-listening to inserting themselves in the conversation, a sudden group of three other men had joined Simon and Nathan. They were all as nude as they were but for the metal between their legs.

The one who spoke had entered pointing at the unique metal between Simon's legs. He looked down to see what him, and soon everyone else was looking at, and noticed a shape carved into the curve. It was subtle and could only be seen in the glow of candlelight but it was there for sure: a little heart pointing down to his tip.

He looked up to see Nathan smirking, "look's like his majesty has a favourite, boys."

The other men leered and chanted at his embarrassment and another put together that this probably indicated who the key around Nicholas' neck belonged to. Another man in the distance said that Simon was in big trouble getting all involved with a man like that. The one voice in the crowd that stood out, however, and silenced the prattish chattering was Kyle's.

"Must be nice," he grunted. Kyle Karn moved to pull the last of his clothes off before he saw everyone looking at him expectingly. He looked around before turning back to Simon and sneering. "He hasn't even made eye contact with the rest of us in months."

"That's 'his majesty' to you," the hero amongst them grunted. Simon Hallow was bad with words and terribly slow on occasion. But where he was sharp, sharper even than his blade, was at chivalry.

Honour. The crowd parted to leave him and Kyle in a circle. The other man walked up, scarily close, and talked right in the Knight's face. If it weren't for their nakedness, Simon thought, then perhaps a fight would have broken out.

"*His majesty*," Kyle spat, "is abusing us."

He walked out into the bathhouse, breaking the circle and sending everyone away to their own self-cleaning.

Simon went a minute later with Nathan where they washed each other's backs in the steamy water.

As they cleaned, they could hear the distant, angry noises of Kyle's attempt at bathing. He was apparently unable to leave his crotch alone during this time in the water and so everyone bore witness to the way he fiddled with himself in his own little corner.

For Simon this time was well spent in conversation and banter. Him, Nathan and a few of the other men had a nice time enjoying the comradery and letting the water wash away their tension.

It seemed like, in his furious attempt at bypassing the cage, Kyle was the only one who couldn't relax. Everyone's head turned in the end to the sound of his exasperated grunting and splashing as he stormed out of the room.

When the knights all got back to their own business, it was Nathan alone who couldn't look away. He spoke morosely on the man who failed to satisfy himself, "he should watch out. Letting his behaviour storm up like that will have him end up the same way Jon did."

And Simon remembered, for the first time since he discarded it, that morbid letter he found in his chamber.

IV

Another week went by in the king's service.

Now involved in the every day at The Dale, Simon had been brought in to stand as a member of the king's guard proper.

Jon's empty spot could go empty no longer, apparently, so it had been during this last week when Simon had started to stand by his monarch's side as often as possible.

At meal times he stood just behind his king's chair with his fellow king's guard, Harold, standing on the other side. There were three other members of the small group, but Harold was the one who mattered most as Nicholas' closest attendant.

The other three rotated and, in down time, made their best efforts to chat and stay friendly. But Harold did not say a word more to Simon than he needed to. The captain of the guard may have been pragmatic but he had his soft spots. Harold on the other hand was just cold. He was no leader, no man interested in raising up his comrades. He was a predator defending his territory hungrily. He told Simon not the necessities but rather the bare minimum, leaving him anxious about his performance.

As it turned out, though, his performance was fine. He found reassurance with those other three guards and together they bonded not only over Harold's icy demeanour but also over sharing tips that the other man had chosen to not tell.

But as it tended to go, when one problem was solved another begun.

As time went on, being in his majesty's presence all day every day, it became increasingly harder not to stare. A problem that spiralled as his tightening cage seemed to only remind him further of the man sat before him.

It wasn't enough anymore to just be in his presence but rather he had to see him always from the corner of his eye. And then he had to look, to so rebelliously stare at him instead. It was an attraction pulled taut by the key nestled comfortably on Nicholas' chest. It was there on that brown cord resting so openly. It had his name etched into it to remind everyone who it was keeping locked up.

But even that was still just a catalyst for the inane lapping up his eyes were doing by the end of the week. He was not just admiring; he was eating up every aspect of his king at any opportunity. The way his ass stretched his trousers tight with each step forward; the fact that the key nuzzled so comfortably in the cleavage of his pecs; pecs that seemed to bounce through his shirt ever so subtly with each step.

It drove him to such a deep madness had had to ask the king to repeat himself when, for the first time since his caging, he spoke to him.

Harold's eyebrows rose inflamed with fury that someone as low as him had dared to ask the king to repeat himself. Nicholas, however, simply did repeat himself, probably used to the affect he had on people.

"I said that today you will be the one to escort me to my chambers. To learn the ropes."

Honoured and confused, Simon quickly nodded his understanding. Waiting boys came in and cleared up and the two men left at the same time, leaving poor Harold alone and a tad flabbergasted.

When they did reach the king's bed chamber, Nicholas didn't leave him to guard the door as he expected he would. In fact he left the door open and, when Simon did nothing but gape inside, he put one finger under the knight's chin and walked him into the room like a dog, pulling him through with just that slight command.

Simon did dare ask what to do or question his king, a trait that Nicholas liked, so he just stood there, straight up, and watched. The king moved slowly across the room to a dresser where he pulled a finely carved chair out into the middle of the room. Even that chair itself looked worth more gold than the knight had ever seen in his life – even more so when Nicholas sat on it.

"Strip."

That was the king's command. As he sat firm on his seat, crossed his arm and raised his head up proudly, he commanded his knight to lose all his clothing. Not wont to make the king repeat himself again, Simon did as he was bade.

He hesitated nervously but just for a second as his obedience overpower his humility.

It took him a few minutes of struggling and clanking about in that armour to get it all off without the help of a squire but he managed it eventually.

The king did not mind the wait, at least he didn't show it if he did. He simply watched expressionless but expecting. And when the underclothes started to come off, and the knights hardened body was exposed to the midday sunlight, he still only observed. Yes, his eyes did wander across his flesh, eyeing up each line that made up his muscles, but it was not a hungry look or a predatory one. Simply an observation of his knight.

When he was finished it took Simon his level best not to move his hands to cover his manhood as he so desperately wanted to. Wearing nothing but a cage ended up feeling more exposed than not wearing anything at all.

Satisfied the king stood up and walked around the back of the chair.

He gestured a hand down at it and commanded once more, "sit."

Simon was weary to in his presence but he obeyed none the less. As he sat down on the surprisingly comfortable cushion atop the wooden furniture, the king went and procured something from a drawer or cabinet he could not see.

And then he touched him.

It was like electricity; that contact from his grace's soft fingers shot through his arm harder than any swordplay could. It made him gasp and caused his skin to tingle joyously. No man had had this affect on him before and so he was starting to realise quite how desperate this cage had made him.

The king, meanwhile was, with great deftness, tying the knight's arms behind the chair. He moved around then, kneeling in front of him, to tie his ankles to the legs of the chair. When Simon finally broke from his reverie he realised the situation he was in. He did not panic. It was the king's will and he trusted him.

Nicholas remained knelt on the floor and looked up. He maintained eye contact as he slowly drew his fingers swirling across the thread of his necklace until they reached the key. He grabbed it between two sultry fingers and lifted it slowly towards the cage between muscled thighs. Simon watched it so intently that all he could see was that key in his mind's eye. Nothing else existed right then.

At last it found its destination. With a soft tap of the metal against the heart on the curve of his cage, the whole thing faded away. The key fell gently to land against Nicholas' chest and the ring that wrapped tightly around Simon's groin remained but the cage on his cock was gone; free now, the appendage wasted no time in springing up for its master.

Simon whimpered at the feeling of finally being free and feeling cool air on it at last. The king too was pleased - smiling for the man at the sight of his eagerness.

Simon's breathy moaning only increased as his owner started tracing gentle fingers up his thighs. He moved his fingertips slowly up and then gently back down when he got dangerously close to his exposedness. The knight reacted not just with his panting but also with the physical movements he could not control. It shamed him, but his legs spread open invitingly as the insides of them were titillated.

"Tell me, sweet king's guard, have you been enjoying your new role?"

Simon couldn't answer beyond an involuntary 'ah' from deep in his throat.

Nicholas moved to finally put his right hand further. While his left remained tracing soft circles on his thigh, the right went to grab and squash and play joyfully with the knight's testicles.

"Have these been feeling heavier, hm?"

Simon started to squirm then as he groaned at the sensation. But when the king whispered, like wind in the meadow, for him to 'shhhhh,' Simon realised that it wasn't a pain but a pleasurable discomfort. When he sat still and let out his moans he realised that the feeling in his balls was nice and suddenly he could not think straight but for the prayers in his head; *oh please crush me your grace!*

One more time he moved up again. His left hand took the right's job by cupping him and his right moved up to grab the shaft and start pumping away. He moved slowly at first, unearthing the glistening tip, before generously – and with a tight grasp – jerking hard.

"I can tell that you have been keeping a very, very, very, very, *very*, good eye on me." He hushed out each 'very' in time to a harder and more intense pump. As glistening liquid began to dribble thicker from the tip and the knight's body began to curl around this centre of pleasure, suddenly Nicholas stopped.

"WAIT!" the knight begged, a raw plea escaping his mouth. But the king heeded him not and instead chose to pull that key up once more. He tapped the cold end of it against the head of Simon's cock and watched joyfully as it began to fall flaccid again.

It shrunk back to its standard size and, once it was done, the cage slowly reappeared around it. Simon squirmed and spread his legs and humped the air, anything to bring back the pleasure that was lost so suddenly. The king stood back up, his arms crossed, and waited for the man to finish his sobbing and calm down.

When he looked back up at him, the monarch answered, "in future, Ser Hallow, you will do well to keep your attention on protecting me rather than staring at me. If you quite think you're capable of that," he snapped his fingers and all the ropes binding Simon fell loose on the floor, "then maybe you'll finally earn that reward."

He turned on his heel and exited the chamber leaving Simon alone, unsatisfied and far worse off than he already was.

V

Simon noticed a change in his behaviour after that day. At first there was a great struggle. He couldn't sleep the entire night after that encounter no matter how tired he got. The feeling just kept him desperately awake. But the night after that, when at last he got some sleep and woke up refreshed, he had started to act differently.

He had started doing more than what was asked of him.

On his rare day off he would join other soldiers in their patrols instead of resting. He would walk the walls or scout the forest edges just to keep on being useful. And on days where he did work he had started acting better, more professional. He hadn't looked at the king out of turn once. No eyes wandered, despite the fact that his thoughts did. But however tight the cage got, he still acted on his best behaviour. He even went beyond on those working days too; just before bed he would always spend another hour working out, whether it be down in the yard or in the privacy of his room.

He was starting to find that this wasn't even draining or troublesome to him – all this extra work – but actually a necessity. For every moment alone and idle was subject to the torture of the cage. If he kept his body busy as well as his mind then he could remedy his situation even slightly.

And of course, in doing that, he would also be improving his service to *him*. He who owned him and he who's attention was gold.

After all., what if he saw? What if he noticed! A reward might be earned this way, attention and favour might be hopefully drip-fed.

Soon that obsession, that need to climax, stopped being a burden as it instead drove him. He did more each day in loyalty to his king.

In council meetings with lords and generals, the fearsome Ser Hallow of the king's guard would glare down those who opposed King Nicholas. He would happen to tighten the grip on Rogue in its sheath whenever a person might object to his majesty's commands. Whenever the king walked up stairs, Simon's arm became the railing he gripped. He even spent one entire night not sleeping and watching diligently over the king. And in true obedience – even though the king was sound asleep – Simon did not look over at him. He stood guard at the foot of the bed, facing away and remaining alert.

All his efforts and all his exertions turned out to be the cure for his night time woes as well. For a day of non-stop work lead to collapse at the end where he would sleep better than he ever had in his life.

But the happiest moment of his recent vortex of victories had to be one isolated moment in the training yard. He was alone, training early during lunch after eating quickly, and saw his grace walking atop the battlements. He didn't watch him; he didn't even turn his head to look. But he did roll his eye just slightly to the side, and just for a split second, to let the knight know that he was being watched and he was being ignored.

He thrust his sword harder after that look, deep into the dummy, as he had to exert the frustration that boiled from the utter pleasure of being denied.

To serve his king made him greatly happy and to work for his favour was a climax like no other.

His fellow knights didn't seem to agree.

The biggest reason for this was brought up by Nathan when he made Simon aware one day that he was the only one of the order actually attracted to men.

"Really?" he asked, shocked, "not one of you find the king attractive."

"Not in the same way you do," he shrugged.

"But... to so willingly wear these cages, to hand yourself over, surely there's a bit of- um- *enjoyment*, being derived?"

Nathan just shook his head before illuminating his friend to the truths of the matter.

"A lot of people here feared that if they said no to the caging the king would simply kill them. Their own fault, really. Some were so desperate for glory and greatness that they simply saw it as one more sacrifice to make on the road to herodom. A lot believed that, as a man, the king would understand the difficulties of a chaste life, and not be so cruel with it all. Boy were they wrong. I mean, some of us haven't had relief for months. And since joining the order, not a single one of us has touched a woman."

"The king started all this on the day of his eighteenth birthday. A great present for himself, he called it. All existing knights were ordered to make the change, to start wearing cages I mean, or else they would lose their positions. And while his reasoning was stated to be that of maintaining loyalty and devotion, the real reason becomes more apparent as each day goes on. He's trying to tame our spirits, keep us focused on nothing but the fight."

Simon swallowed nervously and answered the next part for him, "the fight against the spriggan woods."

Nathan nodded. "He sends reavers to hack trees at the edge of the forest lines or to burn the bushes there. He sends soldiers further out into the country and patrols that work closely with the farmers. War is coming man, any day now. The Dale will march on the spriggan woods soon."

Trumpets blew loud then. A sudden herald came that warned all the knights present in the castle. Simon had never heard it before so Nathan gave him one last piece of education.

"If you hear that tune blowing then it's time to head to the throne room. It's for knights only because it means... it means there's going to be a beheading of one of our lot."

Nathan didn't say any more than that but Simon quickly grasped the rest. It appeared that Kyle had finally gone too far.

VI

The captain looked ashamed.

"Come on man, don't do this, come on." Kyle's voice wasn't begging – he was attempting to implore at the part of the captain he thought knew better. Unfortunately it didn't work.

The captain of the guard continued to tie Kyle up to the 'guillotine' as it was called. It wasn't an actual guillotine but rather a chair with a tall piece of wood standing in front of it. The criminal would be sat on the chair – completely nude – with their ankles tied to the seat legs. That kept their own legs open so that the genitals could be pulled neatly through a hole in the wood where they sat divided from their owner and vulnerable. The hands were tied to the top of the piece of wood and the waist was tied back around the chair keeping them still and exposed. The captain finished tying the last knot as he ignored the soon-to-be-former-knight's braying.

"Shit," Nathan whispered. "I knew he was going to go off but not this bad."

"Now," Simon asked, slightly confused, "when people here say 'beheading.'"

"They don't mean that head," he replied dourly.

And to reassure this point, Vargo had just appeared to take the captain's place near Kyle. He held a large, silver dagger that had been sharpened heavily on one edge. He placed it underneath the exposed balls of poor Kyle and told him to 'shush now' when he sobbed.

Once satisfied with his taunting, he pulled the ring of keys from his waist and slowly fingered his way through each one until he found the key labelled 'Kyle.' He plucked it off the ring and then got down on to one knee where he held it outstretched on the palms of his hands. He bowed his head and waited patiently as Nicholas entered the room and silenced the watching crowd.

He then held his arms out like a showman and addressed the room. "Knights and squires in the Order of the Ram. Today we bear witness to a vile traitor. A man who tried, so pathetically might I add, to take the key to his cage. Luckily, the honourable amongst you ensured that this was brought to my attention." He didn't say a name but his eyes did make contact with the captain's.

In realisation, so did Kyle's as he looked over to his boss, his leader and comrade, with total betrayal. The accused could do no more then look down at his feet ashamed.

The punishment for this, as you all know too well, is beheading!"

To Simon's surprise, a roar erupted from the crowd. He could have sword he was at a football game the way the men whooped at the prospect. He looked around him and saw perhaps two or three others not taking part in the merriment, most notably Nathan. He was just stood, arms crossed and teeth gritted in his set jaw.

"You know the rules, men! You can still prove your innocence by lasting for five minutes. But if you finish before then, you will only be proving the sin in your heart. And you know what happens to sinners!"

"OFF WITH THEIR HEAD!" The crowd shouted back.

"As long as it's not happening to them, eh?" Nathan muttered. Simon just did his best to watch while ignoring the sympathy pains his own groin was already feeling.

The king at last took the proffered key from Vargo, allowing the warlock to stand up again. He moved to be beside Kyle, his hands held respectfully in front of him. In one of them, the dagger that would do the deed rested impatiently. It was called Razor, or so it's said.

"Mercy, your grace," Kyle finally begged, realising the fruitlessness of his pleas. There was no one on his side today. "Mercy, please," he repeated as the key tapped against his cage and allowed his hung dick to fall free.

Regardless of sexuality, even he could not resist the feeling of pleasure brought on by freedom. He'd been in that cage for months, maybe even longer, and now he was free at last. Everyone could see the way he squeezed his eyes shut and tensed every muscle in his body in an attempt to prevent his erection. Unfortunately, his boner still popped up, big and proud for the room to see. Whether from the denial, the sudden exposure or the titillation that came from being so humiliatingly exposed, no one could say, but Kyle's cock had reason to be hard as a brick then.

"Vargo, if you will."

The man nodded at his liege and in his free hand appeared a pocket watch. He held the brass instrument up and nodded back.

"Five minutes," the king confirmed, "are you ready?"

Kyle's tip answered for him. For the king did nothing put slide a teasing finger up the wooden panel towards his exposedness – yet still he started leaking. He decided to move slowly.

He positioned his hand upside down so it stroked over his manhood heel first. His fingers were spread out and as he moved up and up, they curled in to contort to the shape of his testicles and taint. The pads of his fingers, oh so soft, sent small shocks of shivers up his body that actually made tears brim in Ser Karn's eyes.

The knight was looking up at the ceiling, desperately doing his best to prevent the climax that had been building for ages.

As the trailing palm reached his shaft, it squeezed gently, teasing a sad and squeaky "oh god," from Kyle.

As it moved up, the fountain above continued to glaze the phallus in clear, sticky, defeat. Upon reaching the top at last, his hand coated by the fluid, he made his final move. He pushed down, pulling the foreskin and exposing the sensitive red tip. He pushed his palm all the way back down the shaft to leave his trembling and weeping cock on the edge of explosion.

"NO, NO- I CAN'T," Kyle cried, the tears flowing now, "PLEASE, PLEASE! PLEASEEEE!" His last beg was cut off suddenly as he erupted, his seed spilling all over the carpet in thick and heavy ropes.

It was clear by the look on Nicholas' face that he loved this moment. He loved the feeling of power he got when he made people lose the beheading game. Kyle's face was contorted in such a unique expression then as he simultaneously experienced absolution in pure pleasure and the total-end in utter dread.

"About thirty seconds, your grace," Vargo said, putting the pocket watch away.

"Nuh- no..." the trembling voice of the criminal sputtered out as he suddenly felt the cold edge of Razor beneath his balls once again.

The king no longer addressed the room, he instead was looking his victim directly in the eyes now as he said his final word on the matter before leaving – he never liked to stick about for the bloody part.

"Off with his head."

VII

"They'll find some place for him."

Simon hadn't even asked. He had been sat in the dining hall, chewing away distantly at the meat on his plate, when the other man came to join him. He too sat down, food and all, and just started talking.

"The eunuchs usually get sent to the stables. Or the kitchens. Doesn't really matter, to be honest, most end up dying from the infection."

Simon just nodded. He was comforted, all truth be told, that at last it was being spoken about. As soon as everyone had left the scene of the punishment, nobody said a word. It was just back to normal, as if it didn't happen. Probably an attempt to pretend it never happened.

The part that chilled Hallow about the lack of acknowledgment, though, was the niggling reminder in the back of his mind that Jon too had been 'beheaded.' And if this is how little people reacted, then for all he knew Jon's punishment could have happened just five minutes before he came to Draybury.

It made him look at the king differently too. Nicholas was more than just beauty – he was ownership and power. It made him feel cold; like he was sat on the line of sublime submission... or uprising.

"How are you feeling about it?" he asked Nathan.

The other knight shook his head, "I was here since the beginning. The eighteenth birthday, that is. In those five years, I have had the displeasure of seeing what is now thirty-two beheadings."

Simon felt grave hearing that. "Thirty-two too many," he grumbled.

He was worried that that might have been the wrong thing to say then as it was met by silence and a look of appraisal. Finally Nathan did speak again, cutting the tension with his usual friendly smile. "Too right," he agreed.

The two continued to eat wordlessly after that. They silently chewed on the tough meat and let the tensity of the conversation wash over them. Now that it was out there, he felt he could move on from it. He *wanted* to move on from it.

He was ready to leave and start this new chapter he'd been thinking of, when Nathan turned out to be the one to steer the air instead.

He spoke, not making eye contact and talking under his breath. "Come with me," he said, the words coming out like he'd been trying his best to make himself say them for the past five minutes. He did stand up then and Simon nodded, following him through the castle halls.

Tonight was not bath night, which made it both perfect and incredibly risky to host a clandestine meeting in the antechamber. Benches that normally existed to facilitate the changing of the muscle-weary men had now become the seats for the meeting of a secret council.

Simon was surprised not only find three other men there but ones equally as serious as Nathan was. They all sat in a circle on these benches talking in whispers to each other about their honest thoughts on the recent punishment.

While Simon knew not the names of these three other men, he could recognise them as a few in the handful that did not cheer along to Kyle's beheading.

"We're all here today," Nathan lead, "because were sick of seeing that any longer."

"What are you suggesting?" One of the more timid men among them asked, "we could petition for lighter sentences-"

"*Lighter sentences?*" Nathan looked entirely offended. Simon was glad he hadn't uttered his similar thoughts now. "The one who should be sentenced is the king!"

"Shh!" Another man hissed, calming Nathan down. Hallow realised then that these men weren't cowed by the beheading like Nicholas wished them to be. They weren't even angered – they were galvanised to action. From years of discomfort, these men had finally reached the end of a taut tether.

At least they were if they all shared Nathan's strong sentiments.

"Look, men. I enlisted when I was young and hopeful. When our king was but fifteen, and recently grieving the loss of his dads to the spriggans in the woods, I was one of the first there with my sword swearing my service to reclaim the Draybury Dales. I think I can safely speak for everyone here when I say that what we did *not* agree to was a vanity project at the whim of a tyrant's ego!"

"Here, here!" The other men grunted quietly. Simon went along, although his responses were uncertain.

"The first step is to bypass that bloat, Vargo-"

"Sorry," Simon interrupted, "first step?"

"Yes. The first step to overthrowing the king."

Everyone then looked at him and his words in awe, unsure if it was an awe of fear or admiration.

"Look, we can't do anything as long as the man has these locked up," he grabbed at his cage in his trousers when he said that, "so listen here, I've been-"

He stopped then to look around, nervous of listeners. He crouched down and the other men did the same. He whispered from here on, "I've been meeting with a sorcerer in the town. He says he's heard of our, ah, curse. He knows how to undo it and will grant us our freedom for but a half-gold each."

Fifty silver was not an unreasonable amount to have tucked away – what shocked the guards was exactly whether or not the sorcerer could do as he had promised.

"I believe him," Nate insisted, "when I asked for proof he pulled out a cage, an empty one. Says he liberated a poor trapped man a long while ago."

"And it was one of Vargo's cages?" An uncertain man asked.

"Well," he said, starting to get antsy, "not exactly... BUT it looked similar to one of the king's!" He pointed then at the groin of a confused Simon. "His has that heart near the slit. The cage that the sorcerer procured, that one had runes running up the curve. The similarity was striking, I'm certain of it!"

Everyone seemed to nod then, although it may have been a self-delusion rather than an assurance.

Simon put a hand on Nate's shoulder then, and looked him square in the eyes. "Listen, brother. That is not what you need to be certain of."

Nathan looked back with steel in his eyes. "Ask me."

"Are you certain you want to go down this path? That 'kingslayer' is the ugly mark you wish to bear?"

"I am. In fact," he stood up then, proud, "I do not only believe that Nicholas is unfit but also that a new man needs to sit the throne at Drayburyshire. The midlands need to be united against the ghosts of giants and push back down to reclaim the island's south. That won't happen as long as we keep entertaining the whims of a man who can't let go of his treasures from Neroma!" He held his arms spread to indicate that he was referring to the bathhouse.

Everyone else stood up to join him, empowered by his words. "What do we have to do," asked the man who was merely a timid bystander minutes ago.

"If you are in for sure then meet in three days by the gate. At the witching hour. The green knight will be on watch duty then and that man is more than sympathetic to our cause. He'll let us out then we will go, find the sorcerer and free our manhoods."

"And after that?" Simon asked.

"We return. And we don't leave the castle again until one of us bears the mark of 'kingslayer.'

VIII

To commit a coup one must first have total and utter determination to overthrow their king. And right then, during his evening duty as king's guard, Simon had never felt more devotion to his master.

He was mixed with shock and elation when he was told the news of his posting – a feeling soon stung by his sense of betrayal. For he was so totally excited to do this for his king that he felt like he was a traitor to Nathan's cause.

But this job was one he had been dreaming off since that metal first cradled him. It was one scenario, one fantasy, amongst many that had kept him awake while he humped pathetically at a pillow.

His king had instructed him to stand guard while he made use of the bathhouse.

"Yessir!" Was Simon's eager response. The king only looked back at him with those expressionless eyes, like the knight he was looking at was nothing more than a dog barking.

When the two entered, Simon was told to wait by the bath. He did, and Nicholas came out a few minutes later, a towel wrapped around him. Wrapped very low around him. As he walked into the room, Simon traced the path of his V-line down to where the treasure was concealed. As he walked by, the knight then made eyes at the dimples in his back that heralded the beautiful buttocks concealed beneath the fabric.

He swallowed nervously, knowing that the king had done this purposefully – just for him.

It must be a trap, he thought. Was the king weeding out the weaker knights before battle? Was Ser Hallow to be next for the beheading? Razor flashed in his mind and he shuddered.

He ended up forgoing any fears though, instead indulging in the sight before him – the all encompassing importance of his life; rex pulchra.

The Beautiful Man Without Mercy

For Nicholas, oh man of marble, had let his towel fall from his waist. As he stepped lightly down the steps and into the water, he became one with the baths and transformed into an oil painting.

The ripples of liquid, the swirls of steam, and the way both kissed his skin, made a landscape titled 'handsome.'

It was enough to kill Simon just running his vision up his king's legs – all elegance in masculinity. It was power enough to take his breath; the way his grace's behind was soft in its strength. And to dull the mind was to be that manhood of shining light between his majesty's legs.

The king's visage was statuesque – primarily in size. Simon might once have thought a penis so small would be a disappointment but here, on a being like that, it was virtue untold. It was the manhood of a hero, of a warrior of a conqueror! It was the cock – so elegant, so lithe – of an angel of death. The knight saw in his mind's eye the vision of Nicholas walking amongst a battlefield in his nudity and still being twice the man as any armoured knight. For he was soft death and loving eternity. Afterlife in life.

Just twenty minutes passed before the king decided to exit the waters. Simon stared still, unashamed and uncaring if it lead even to torture.

He watched his liege dry himself gently with the retrieved towel. He watched his liege do so in a way that conjured up whole new images of his body; his arms flexed as he moved; his legs tensed as he stretched and bent over; and lord did his ass stun as the towel squashed up the muscles and jiggled the perfection of it all.

When Nicholas was done, he looked back over his shoulder at his observer.

"Do you want to taste?"

Simon answered by drooling. The king laughed at him.

"You know, I asked you to guard me here tonight not just because I trust your, ah, watchful eye, Ser Hallow..." he walked over and teased open the drawstrings of the man's breeches. It was too hot in the room to wear armour and not faint, so the knight had only been in his underclothes. Now he was just in his shirt, both his bottoms and sword falling to the floor under the king's command.

Nicholas then produced, apparently left nearby, the key to Simon's cage. He generously tapped the top of it, letting him free. Just like the imprisoned Kyle's had, his cock shot up immediately. It had already drawn dampness onto the front of his clothes from his staring and now, unearthed, it practically streamed that sad little liquid from its sensitive head.

"What can I do for you, your grace?" his words weren't his own. It wasn't a conscious answer, just a breath escaping. It was what he needed to say to earn more favour, the virus of seduction steering his head.

"I need to divine some information about certain... *rebels*."

The king pressed himself against Simon as he said that. There was a warm pressure on his dick now as it rubbed gently against Nicholas' abs.

Don't answer. Lie. Run. The knight's mind went wild with fear at being caught out. But his body was of another. He thought that he should stay silent, but his hips needed nothing else than to thrust against its master's belly. Simon tried to splutter out some words, any words – perhaps a question in answer to steer away from this folly of rebellion – but the king had come to cradle his balls. That was the final stand that melted his brain from sensible thought.

He existed now solely to cum.

His body was a machine borne to seek the pleasures of King Nicholas' hands. He slid up and down the sweaty abs, slick with his semen, as his body thrust involuntarily. He curled around that point of pleasure, making it his centre, and the king looked up to pull their faces very close. He moved them closer even, putting his free hand on the back of Simon's neck. He pulled them merely inches apart. But did not kiss. There needed no kiss – just breath in exchange; souls mingling in sensation.

Finally, the knight answered. His words came out of his mouth in the same manner as his seed did. They gushed hard, fast, thick and in copious amounts before giving a few final sputtering gasps.

"NATHANNATHANNATHAN! HE. I. NATE. THEY ALL. REBELS. AH...ah... It's Na-Nathan."

He divulged everything then. As he came down from the high of his ejaculation, he spilled every detail of the little meeting and the sentiments going around some of the knight's heads.

At last the king thanked him. He tapped the key against the exhausted tip and smiled to see it wrapped up in metal again. When Simon looked down at it, he saw that the heart was no longer a subtle engraving. Instead it was a gold shape, clearly and boldly etched into the cage.

"You're loyalty will be remembered, Ser. Should your information provide fruitful then perhaps you'll get that taste you want so desperately." The king hummed before leaving. If he had stayed then he would have seen Simon weep.

IX

It's happening again.

And this time it's my fault.

The horns blew in the courtyard the next day just before lunch. It was a sound similar to the trumpets that heralded a beheading but with a slightly different tune.

Either way it brought dread down Simon's spine as he finally caught on to what he had done. What he had done to Nathan.

He was relieved, at least, to see that the guillotine, as it were, was not dragged out to the throne room this time.

The knights all stood, in that same circle of eager attention, around the centre where his majesty was besides Vargo.

The ring of keys hung at his waist but now Razor was sheathed in the belt of his grace instead. Instinctively, Simon rested his hand on his own trusted blade; letting Rogue comfort him.

"It saddens me deeply to have to summon yet another tribunal so soon after the last. But another crime has been committed, one far worse than the last. We can only thank God that it was brought to my attention before it got out of hand." The king did not look towards the source of information this time and so Ser Hallow let himself exhale.

He had been nervous that he might be exposed, mainly for the fact that those other three knights were in the crowd – the members of Nathan's rebellion – and they were all eyeing each other nervously. Notably, Nathan was not present.

Neither was the green knight.

The former's absence was soon explained, though, when he bewas dragged through the door by the captain of the guard.

He moved ashamedly: head down and hands tied behind his back. Once in the centre, the captain pushed him down where he fell to his knees before Nicholas, his hands still bound.

"This man has been found guilty of treason." He said the next word with thunder in his voice – much so that it shook the hearts of each man in the crowd. Even Vargo looked uncomfortable.

"*Regicide.*"

The circle widened subtly as everyone unconsciously shifted away from Nathan. He still didn't look up from the ground.

"He was found attempting to remove his cage with help from some sort of street practitioner. Before we dole out punishment, men, why don't we check this so-called practitioner's credentials?"

That whipped Nate's head up. He looked sharply around the room to see what the King had meant and saw, like everyone else, that the captain had disappeared again. Only now he returned with a man – unbound – who looked rather sorry.

"Testify," the king commanded.

"Muh-my liege! I am your humble serv-"

"*Now.*"

The man gave a dry swallow.

"My name is Plutarch-"

"Your real name not your fucking wizard name."

"Paul Burtenshaw, your grace." He mumbled.

"And are the claims true, Mr Burtenshaw, that you can indeed break one of my cages?"

The man was so terrified he was shaking on the spot. Nicholas walked over and unsheathed Razor, letting the steel sing in the air.

"NO! N-no I cannot, your grace."

"You showed us," Nathan growled, "you promised." Animal backed into a corner; he bit at the air.

"Well?" Nicholas asked the man.

"I- I did indeed do that. But the cage I showed them was magic from elsewhere, by another hand. I do not, nor does anyone, possess the talent to break a cage of your design. I was merely attempting to swindle these knigh- ACK!" His voice splattered out of his mouth in blood as the king thrust Razor through the man's stomach. The blood left a smattering on the king's neck and up half of his face but he chose to let it sit there as the sorcerer bled out on his throne room carpet.

He moved back then to challenge Nathan. On his way, he made the swift movement to cut the knight's bonds and let his hands free.

Nate did not move. He just looked up at his liege waiting to hear the verdict.

"Remember, boys, that to betray me is to betray your selves." He sheathed Razor at his hip again and looked over to the warlock. The man came over, knelt down, and presented a key in his palms.

"For a crime as high as this one, Nathan Smith, you are sentenced to absolvement."

The tandem of sharp, scared onlookers breathing in at the same time washed over the room like a grave wind. Simon was the only one not aware of what absolvement entailed. He watched the scene unfolding before him with great attention, sure that it can't be worse than a beheading.

Nicholas retrieved the key from Vargo, who moved back away again, and held it loosely in his hand to tease the locked up prisoner.

"Any last words?" he asked.

Nathan had nothing to say. He just stared listlessly back up at the king, life draining from his eyes with every second that passed by as he slowly accepted his fate.

"Fine." He lifted the key to hold it upright in front of his face. "Nathan Adams, I hereby absolve you."

He blew gently on the key then, his soft lips pushing a gentle wind over the tool. As he did, the key started to turn to dust. From the top down, it dissolved into the air until the king stopped his blowing and nothing was left in his open hand.

Absolvement, Simon realised. *Absolved from his pleasure. The man may have well had become a eunuch.*

Doomed forever to never take his cage off, Nathan became a very empty and emotionless man before everyone's eyes.

The king walked over to him, "you will now serve no one but the war – no feelings but for the fight. Do you understand me?"

Noone was looking at him now though. For a rare moment, the king was the second most interesting person in the room as all heads turned to wonder what the absolved knight might do. He had no reason to serve now, no master who could reward him. He could fight, lash out or kill even in sudden furious vengeance.

But when Nicholas reached him, and he gripped the hair of the absolved to tilt his head back and look up at him in the eyes, the man only had one thing to say.

"Yes sir."

X

No one could say that King Nicholas was not a man of his word.

On the same night as the absolvement, Simon was once again asked to escort his liege up to his chamber for the night.

Once they entered, the king placed him to stand in the centre of the room where he could watch as he removed his jewellery and any other outer layers of clothing until he was stood in just his shirt and trousers.

Then he backed up, back towards Ser Hallow, where he nestled right up to him as he whispered in sultry tones. He moved one hand up behind to cup the knight's face so gently.

"You helped me a lot today, good ser. I think it's time for that reward I promised."

He didn't wait for thanks or agreement from him, the king simply bent over as he undid the laces on his breeches before pulling them down. The movement was agonisingly slow as he bared himself and rubbed his behind against Simon's caged dick. When he stood up straight again, kicking his trousers away but not bothering to remove his shirt, he looked back over his shoulder to invite.

"I know how hungry you've been since the day you arrived, hero," he cooed.

In fact, Simon liked him this way more than total nakedness. Being bottomless only highlighted the important areas and escalated his beauty. The way he stood as well, leaning on one leg, pushed the shape of his ass into something statuesque. And the shirt slightly covering the top made the mind crazy, made him want to lift it up so he could bear witness to the entirety of this perfection.

He got down on one knee then, so his face was level with his desire, and then hunched just a bit more so he could trail up to his prize. He dragged the tip of his nose up the back of Nicholas' left thigh, slowly leading his way up to his gorgeous butt. When he reached the plump curve, he let his lips trail over the soft skin before finally planting one reverent kiss.

He could no longer hold back, no longer savour. He kissed again and then again, switching cheeks occasionally but still planting dozens of soft, exuberating worships across the beauty.

He started to lick next, desperate to taste, and was not disappointed by how his salty sweat shocked his tongue. It was everything and it was focus. In sweet obsession he groped as he continued to orally worship, unable to let go of this divinity. He cradled and grabbed and squashed and held on as tightly as he could as soon he started to bite as well, hungry for more from the delicious rear.

When at last he was sure of his permission – and slightly not caring if it earned him reprimand anyway – he moved into the middle. He took the king's ass in both his hands and spread the pillows apart to claim the real treasure.

Tight and pink and smooth.

He dove in unable to admire for too long without holding back. He licked and licked and tasted heaven with each. He stuck in further, his head nuzzled firmly between the buttocks, desperate to live his entire life in this haven.

The only thing to snap him out of his joy was the realisation that the king had been quiet the entire time. No mock nor approval. He had just been stood there, letting Simon indulge in his deepest desire.

He wasn't even erect himself. Whatever sensations the worship was causing hadn't brought on any arousal for Nicholas.

This worship wasn't for his benefit, it was Simon's reward.

For my service I earn the opportunity to worship.

He knew this fact in his mind... but that didn't mean he could physically stop himself. He knew that the king was an evil man, that he never denied, but now it was time he acknowledged his own alignment.

Because he had started to come to the realisation that not only did the king love dominating he had trained his men to love being dominated.

As he ran through the facts he carried on with the meal. With every dark realisation, he still tasted another bead of electric sweat that rewired his mind with devotion.

He wanted to hate the king, he thought, but his body wanted to love him. Right there, on his knees with his face buried in the man's ass, he was battling with light and dark. Devotion to this evil man was evil in itself, but how bad could evil be if it was this beautiful – if reverence of it tasted this good.

I need him.

I hate him.

He finally stopped, drool dribbling down his chin as he pulled away, when the muscles in his tongue and jaw became too tired to carry on.

"Satisfied?" the king asked, turning around and looking down at him. He ran his hands through the knight's hair, rustling it and petting him like a cat who he'd just given a treat.

It was an action that brought great anger to Simon's heart – not in itself but anger at the fact he loved it. A self-loathing at the fact that his cock, which was leaking like a waterfall, is so telling him that all he needs in life is to obey this handsome man.

After he nodded his delight, the king dismissed him. Still, he needed to reflect on his thoughts.

He took to walking the castle grounds in the cold night air to ponder his musings. As he walked he reminded himself of the absolvement and of the beheading. He remembered the warning that the green knight had given him on the first day – and wondered where exactly that rebellious man had gotten to now. He thought on the other men, all heterosexual but still at the whim of his chastity cages. He thought of war and of peace and of Nathan's speech before. And in-between each of these, he was torn back to the side of rapture by the taste that lingered on his tongue and on his lip.

The nectar taste of *him*.

His stroll came to an end once he reached the horses and realised it was probably about time to try and sleep. He knew tonight would be a restless one as the last of his king's sweat danced across his taste buds.

He was surprised to see someone besides a guard, however, when he looked over to see a stable hand at work. He had hair long, brown and wavy to his neck. His face had a rough beard and his eyes were a dull grey. He was brushing the horses, but he did so slowly as if energy had escaped him completely. Simon stared for a moment, unable to place why he was fascinated with this zombie of a man.

Then he turned to look back at him and Simon saw chiselled features beneath the unkempt visage.

And he saw past and saw who this man really was.

He remembered the letter and the 'guillotine' and he remembered, as he looked now into his eyes, poor Jon Tennant. The man who willingly gave it all to be free of this service.

Jon nodded at Simon.

Simon nodded back.

He had been battling between the outward evil and personal good 'til now, but seeing the man who was once in his position made him realise what service to the king could drive people to do.

Self-destruction. The ruin of the world around you. No. He decided then that the king had to die.

87

XI

It was around three days later, once more in the night time, when Simon at last took action.

He was tired, dreadfully so, from twisting and turning in his sheets – this time not from repressed arousal. He would be lying if he said it was non-existent, though. In that sweet moment where he ebbed between his treasonous thoughts and the embrace of sleep he would think unwillingly of the king's body. Specifically, one large part of it. Then he would snap back awake, angry at himself for falling back into the trap of loving him.

It was at the witching hour, when at last he gathered the courage to stalk up to the king's bed chamber alone.

Where others may have faltered, he was incredibly glad to find that none other than Harold was the one guarding the king's door that night.

A sweet appetizer.

"Hark, Ser Hallow, what do you think you're doing at this time of night?"

"I'd like to see his grace," he said stoically. Harold narrowed his eyes. As soon as he moved to rest his hand on the hilt of his blade, Simon moved swifter to unsheathe Rogue.

Panic danced in Harold's eyes for a moment as he comprehended and quickly switched from resting on to pulling out his blade. He was a second slower than Simon but that was no reason to fight dirty. They both waited for one another to be prepared before entering a duelling stance.

The two waited for the other to pounce, their faces both getting tenser with each second, though Harold's growling was stronger.

"I will protect the king," he seethed, "I love him!"

"No," Simon sighed. "You don't."

He blocked deftly when the raging man charged. The sound of the metal filled the air in the same way the reflection of candlelight on steel did. It was sharp, confusing and harrowing. It played a steel medley that Simon hoped to all gods would not wake up Nicholas.

One thing he was certain about from the start of it all was that he'd win this fight. Harold was talented – having earned his position – but he was no captain of the guard. He was no hero of the seven kingdoms.

And his blade was not forged in dragon scale.

It shattered, jagged shards of metal falling to the carpet, as Rogue's relentless swiping finally broke the steel.

Still not relenting, though, the man blocked the door with his body in some faux-noble attempt at self-sacrifice.

"You would have to kill me befo-"

Simon beat him over the head with the flat of his blade. The man fell the floor in an unconscious thump.

He checked that the knight was not bleeding before he moved at last to enter his destination. It felt wrong, evil, bad, treasonous and most wicked to walk into this room without express permission. As he pushed the door open and stepped across the threshold, his cock started to twitch and feel small, like even asleep the king was reprimanding him.

This is exactly why you're here, he reminded himself, *he cannot have power like that.*

He walked over to the bed, his blade still unsheathed, and stood at the foot, hovering like a wraith. He looked down to see his king asleep. Vulnerable.

He was naked, wrapped in soft purple silk. His sheets seemed to tangle with his limbs like a sea of grace – another painting to hang in the gallery of Nicholas' perfection.

Simon stared, looking down at the king's dick. Free, uncaged and resting as soft and elegant as ever.

As he continued to hesitate, his senses ended up losing the battle of will. Not only was the magnificent sight one to halt his blade, it was every pleasure of the man.

The scent of his lingering odour – he had not bathed today and that natural smell hit Simon's brain like a rush.

The sound of his gentle exhales in sleep was a calming breeze that made his heart flutter with affection – suddenly a new side was seen as the king seemed cute in this state of sleep.

As for the touch of him, the taste of him, Simon was already far too familiar. Now he wanted nothing more than to indulge those senses again.

Focus, man, he groaned internally. He looked around the room to find anything that might draw his attention before he attempted again to lunge into the act.

He saw Razor on the dresser, wrapped in its blue and gold sheathe. He imagined then what it would be like to take it and cut off the king's genitals, to leave him there bleeding out at his own beheading.

He only felt guilt from that.

There was no vindication in killing him, he realised. He stood there, Rogue in hand, and imagined every which way he could kill, maim and destroy King Nicholas, but none brought satisfaction.

He is evil, he moaned in his mind.

Another monster beheaded at the blade of a hero.

But that still left him unsatisfied. Still left him caged, he realised. He saw then the key on the king's neck, still dangling on that brown thread.

He could take it – kill him and take it! He would be free, the kingdom would be free.

He would be free. He would be *free*.

I don't want freedom.

Simon might have pushed himself to kill the king in another world but there was no realm in perception wherein Ser Hallow would let go of his cage.

Denial, sweet denial. Power over others, yes, but power over him? *Yes*. He loved to love too much.

He decided then, in putting his sword softly to the ground, that this man having power over the world was a worthwhile sacrifice... as long as it meant he still had power over him.

He suddenly didn't care about Kyle Karn, Nathan Smith or Jon Tennant. They were losers in the game he was winning by being the loyal servant of this man.

His attention was the prize he won.

That being said, he still froze up when the king shuffled in his bed, starting to awaken.

He panicked as he realised he might just lose it all then for being caught where he was not permitted.

The king saw him though and sighed softly.

"There he is," he said rubbing his eyes. His voice was low, deep and sleepy, "I was just dreaming of you."

He sat up on his elbows and raised one foot from the silk tangles. The sheets fell off him like spring water as one soft leg lifted in the air. Simon knelt down so that he could take the heel of the foot with his left hand and tilt it down with his right so that he may plant a kiss on the top of his foot.

It was a seal. A contract signed of devotion. Simon forwent any of his betrayal as he signed his love to the king.

Pleased, Nicholas spoke a last time, "join me now. Protect me in sleep, Ser Hallow." He let his body fall gently back into slumber, curled in the bed.

Simon, understanding his meaning, stripped himself to match the king's nudity. He slipped into the bed with him and wrapped his thick arms tightly around the man. The king teased him by pushing his ass against the caged cock and Simon was grateful to be a recipient of his cruelty once more.

And what if he walked in the ash of the world? Simon would gladly lead armies to ruin just to earn a cold glance from this man who loved in idolatry.

XI

Reward had been given dutifully, as the king was like to do, for Simon's final devotion.

He had now been moved from his own chambers to permanently sleep in the soft bed of his majesty. Every night the two would embrace, nude and hot and becoming one.

It was always at Nicholas' discretion though what position they took. On most nights they would take that original spooning position that so defined them. Sometimes the king would prefer to be facing the knight. Sometimes he chose to lay on top of him making pillows of his chest. Some nights he simply wished for solitude and would take half the bed on his own leaving Simon untouched.

But whatever they did, the knight was always grateful. Each night he got to crawl under the covers was another night he said a silent prayer to whatever god had granted him this joy.

And it was sweetened further by the knowledge that Harold had still been placed on guard duty. He was forced most nights to stand outside the king's chamber knowing that he was guarding Simon also.

He had of course raised his complaints initially. He pointed wearily to his broken sword and cursed Simon's bloodline to the king's face. Nicholas however just pointed at the shards of the broken sword and commanded Harold to clean it up.

The guard went silent immediately before mumbling a 'yes your grace' as he got on his hands and knees to collect the pieces. The king walked on and the matter was never heard of again.

In fact, the king had deigned to keep Simon in his presence 24/7 soon enough. Simon now not only slept and rose with him but also dined with him three times a day and bathed with him each night. He had not earned any more 'rewards' in all that time and in fact it only made his passions, his virilities, more potent. And that made him even more grateful. He was the one the king wanted to torture; he was the one the king loved to see squirm. It was an honour to be his plaything.

As time went on the war councils increased in frequency too. Soon lords, ladies, generals and captains from all across the county were in attendance at The Dale as they drew up plans to strike at the spriggans.

Each meeting was locked and clandestine. These plans and operations were so important that not even waiting staff nor knight could stand in the room. The gentry entered with their king and they spoke in solemn secrets.

Of course, the exception was Simon. The king insisted, risked the war even, on Simon being present. He said he would have no battle without his loyal man at his side. Begrudgingly, the others accepted at last that there would be no war without coming to terms with this - so they met and they counselled and Ser Harrow stood behind his liege's seat each time.

In the last week that went by, about three different people in that room were hanged. No concrete proof had been given of them leaking any information, but the king took the matter so seriously that even a whiff of misbehaviour was grounds for death. Simon also suspected that perhaps it may have been a bit of a deterrent.

But in all of the time that passed and plans that went forward, there was still one matter that no one could seem to solve.

"The green knight," Vargo said one morning at breakfast. He had come into the dining hall while Nicholas and Simon were enjoying a continental.

"My spies believe that by now he has fled Drayburyshire all together."

"Your spies are wrong," was all he said in return not even looking up from his croissant.

Vargo wasn't sure how to respond to that. He looked to Simon for help – the two becoming quite friendly now that he was in the inner circle – but the hero had no ideas either.

"A-and you're sure about that, your grace?"

He nodded, "I am. In fact, never mind Drayburyshire, never mind even Draybury, the man hasn't left The Dale."

"I suppose," the warlock considered, "that if he was still so close than my spies would have missed him. They have been fanning out as time went on, not suspecting he'd remain nearby."

"Good, then catch him," the king command, still finding his berries and pancakes more interesting than this conversation.

"It may take-"

"I will have him by midnight." Simon interrupted the warlock. He knew this was a distraction for the king – the war effort came first. He would swat this fly so his majesty could return to ruling.

Nicholas finally did look up then, his icy stare looking into the knight's golden eyes. "I should hope so," he replied before returning to his meal.

Simon continued eating as well, leaving Vargo in somewhat of a stunned silence.

"I-if that is the matter laid to rest then... I have one more request."

"What?"

"Of Simon." The king didn't care, silent now that the conversation wasn't about him.

"What is it?" The man in question asked. "How can I help?"

"If I might... I would like to appraise your blade."

"Rogue?" Simon lifted his scabbard and walked around the table to hand it to the warlock. "Why are you interested in Rogue?"

The man seemed to soften as he took the blade and unsheathed it; like being in it's presence made him vulnerable.

"It is an ancient device," he said with awe. "I simply wanted to say hello."

Simon leant to whisper to Nicholas, "um, does he normally talk to swords."

"Probably," the king replied, "probably fucks them too."

"Right." Simon held his hand back out to reclaim his blade from the other man. This seemed to displease Vargo as he reluctantly sheathed it and gave it over.

"Take care of him," he said.

"I will," Simon nodded. The warlock walked off then, leaving the two men alone again.

"Worry not," the king said, "that was most likely just Vargo showing he cares for you. My little dragon is weird like that sometimes, just be grateful."

"Grateful, my liege?"

The king smirked. "Yes. That you are now one of us men whose name's will be written in the annals of history."

XII

The king ate alone at lunch that day and again then at tea time. It had grown dark outside and while he knew that his man would deliver before the clock struck twelve, he was starting to grow impatient.

When at last he grew sick of pacing back and forth, he decided he would head down the dungeons where he would wait for Simon Harrow to return with his quarry. He traced the walls of his castle as he went down stone brick stairs, humming to himself as he went. He had rarely ever walked through these walls alone in his life, always having Vargo, the captain or Harold at his side. Now all he ever wanted there was Simon. So he moved alone, down, down to the dungeons.

As he went deeper and the air grew staler and the walls bore more and more moss, he started to feel alive.

Down here was where the dead rotted while the living residents awaited the same fate. It filled him with vigour. He would be certain to play with his little toy knight that evening, he thought, high on the feeling.

As he took another step closer to the dank rooms, he toyed more and more with different ways to twist his man into wishing he was nothing more than furniture to be sat on.

Hm.

And speaking of the devil, just as the king made his last step down into the torchlit chambers deep beneath the earth, Simon too walked in. He had come from the outer entrance to drag the green knight to his shackles ready for his grace.

"Well met," Nicholas appraised, making the knight smile wide. "Why is he naked?"

"O-oh. Well I thought he might do with some humility as I dragged him through the village."

The king smiled proud, "I see. And tell me, was he stirring rebellion? Trying to rise up pitchforks against the castle?"

"Not even," he said looking down at the sad, sobbing man he had chucked to the ground. Joshua apparently had stopped putting up a fight once he was stripped, too focused on trying to cover every inch of his skin to do any kind of thrashing. "The man was just trying to tell the people how woeful it was being a knight in service to you, that it was torture to serve The Dale."

"And did they listen?"

"Of course not. It was a bit pathetic actually, watching him get chucked out of every public house around because the people wouldn't hear a word against the man who would liberate the woods."

The king was pleased to hear that indeed.

Simon then lugged the green knight by his arm back up to his feet and dragged him even deeper into the bowels of the castle. He took him past cages filled with skeletons or other gaunt looking men.

Somewhere near the back, he chucked him into an empty cell. He was ready to lock it and leave it be but the king had other plans.

He raised a hand to stop Simon, "hold. This man was a knight. To betray the order, well, you have seen how I treat those that break my trust."

Simon looked down at Joshua and wondered whether it'll be beheading or absolvement. Either way, it made his heart tingle this time to imagine the mighty Nicholas doling out punishment. *He deserves it*, he thought looking down at him.

"Chain him to the ceiling," the king commanded. Simon obeyed, moving to grab Joshua's wrists to tie them above his head, leaving him dangling from the roof. Still, he didn't fight back. He just looked down at the ground humiliated.

The knight stepped back then, allowing his grace to do his work.

He held up his right hand to Joshua, "you were bitching because of what? Denied pleasure? That's what you really want, eh?" As he spoke, black lines began to appear on his fingers, wrapping like snakes across his hands and up under his sleeves.

"Then I shall give you as much pleasure as you like." Once the black lines grew up out of his collar again to draw up across his face, he moved his hand towards the bare stomach of Joshua.

The green knight was paying attention now, staring with shaking eyes at the spell.

Once his palm had touched the man's belly it rested there for just a second. As Nicholas closed his eyes, breathing in, his hand passed through the man's stomach.

It pushed palm first into his body until it was entirely inside him. He squirmed and groaned and tried to wriggle free from the strange phasing – all too late.

The king's wrist went through as well and once he was deep enough inside he started to search, his hand feeling inside the green knight's body.

He stopped suddenly when he found the treasure.

At the same time Joshua let out a pathetic squeak.

Suddenly, the king's arm tensed and rippled as he closed his hand into a fist around something.

The stripes on his body then moved backwards from where they came, going across his skin to travel through his arm and his hand and into whatever it was that he had taken a hold of.

He pulled his hand back then and out of the man's stomach. It exited his body just as the tattoos disappeared fully.

The king exhaled.

Joshua was left exactly the same way as before it appeared but now he was squirming in his restraints as his hips seemed to move on their own.

He was also letting out a series of grunts and moans under his breath.

"Ah, ooh, ugh, ah- my lord! God, please, god- ahhhhhh."

"Let him down now," Nicholas said. Simon did, unlocking the cuffs and letting the green knight fall free to his knees.

The man didn't run or fight though, he instead leant back against the wall, still on his knees, and spread his legs open as wide as they went as he stared at his caged dick.

"Oh pleaseeeeee, oh- oh- oh, PLEASE," he groaned until finally he shot ropes of seed across the grey floor. His face showed bliss.

But only for a moment.

"W-wait- hooo, okay, hooo, please tha- that's enough!" he complained.

"What did you do?" The knight asked his king.

"I found that special spot that all men have inside them," he shrugged, "and then I placed a curse on it. He will now experience pure orgasm until he dies."

Simon looked down and witnessed this. Joshua, in his shaking and shuddering, was now clawing at the stones, his body writhing as he begged it to stop. He squirted next all over the floor, clear liquid spraying from his cage relentlessly. Even after that finished, his body continued to shake in pleasure.

He moved forward from his position to his hands and knees. He tried his best to crawl towards Nicholas but did not even make it halfway as his wobbling limbs fell from under him.

Soon his groaning became shouts of agony and discomfort. The two men watched this poor zombie do his best to move under his now shaken body but he could not even stand anymore. In the end, Joshua became nothing but a whimpering pile of muscle unable to escape the puddle of his own fluids.

Simon exhaled, "that was..."

"Beautiful," Nicholas finished for him. "I might try that trick on you tonight," he hummed.

Simon just nodded, "I would be honoured."

The king smiled at his knight's willing. "Worry not, I won't curse yours eternally. We wouldn't want to lose my best knight."

Simon shook his head, "no, my liege, if that is your wish then I am disposable."

The king opened his mouth to respond but instead was quiet. Simon was quite shocked to see that, for the first time since meeting him, Nicholas had a display of emotion on his face other than sadism. He moved his hand up to cup his knight on the cheek.

"You are anything but," he explained. "You are not here to die for me, good Ser. That is my warlock, my captain, my king's guard's jobs. You are here to live for me."

Simon swallowed nervously, "my king..."

"I had only started this war, that I had been harking on about for years now, because I had someone that I love beside me to fill me with confidence. Yes, the other knights serve me and wear their cages but you," he took his free hand and cupped the groin of his man, "you want to serve me. You would willingly wear the cage if even you had the key in hand. I only have power over you, because you let me, do you understand?"

As the war ignited around them and lesser men burned every day, what else did Simon have to say right there, on the eve of chaos, than,

"I love you too."

For more from the KEYHOLDER series

Head to @lewiskingauthor on social media.

About the author

Lewis King is an English author writing stories for other gay men like himself to enjoy – things that mix both an appreciation of good, fantasy storytelling with spicy queer romance.

Also from Phoenix Wings Publishing

The Daughters of God by Phoenix Clarke

DARK FANTASY/THRILLER STORY

Read the blurb here >>>

"Ancercy is the fatal disease spread to mankind when they sleep with daemons.

While the south of an otherwise unremarkable kingdom becomes embroiled in an epidemic of this foul affliction, and those within seek the desperate cure, there are those without who are working to hasten the spread of ancercy.

And with the mayor's son starting to be turned away from parlour doors, even the queen has taken time from her daughter's baptism to attend to the matter; a baptism through which the future of this very kingdom will be told in smoke and water.

A future at whim to the designs of witchers and the commands of clergy - a kingdom of ambitious men. But not one made without the decisions of three women in particular: the magister, the whore and the princess... the daughters of God."

Head to phoenixclarke.co.uk for more info or buy now on amazon in paperback, hardback and kindle + KU.